The Lucky Lizard

The Lucky Lizard

ELLEN A. KELLEY

ILLUSTRATED BY Kevin O'Malley

young Readers
who 'love books

DUTTON CHILDREN'S BOOKS ✦ *New York*

Text copyright © 2000 by Ellen A. Kelley

Illustrations copyright © 2000 by Kevin O'Malley

CIP Data is available.

Published in the United States by Dutton Children's Books,
a division of Penguin Putnam Books for Young Readers
345 Hudson Street, New York, New York 10014
www. penguinputnam.com

ISBN 0-525-46142-6
Designed by Alan Carr
First Edition • Printed in USA
1 3 5 7 9 10 8 6 4 2

To John, Sean, Anne, Anita, and The Group,
whose love and encouragement have made me
the luckiest writer in the world —E.A.K.

The Lucky Lizard

Lots of humans think lizards just lie on rocks in the sun all day. But Todd Boucher, the kid I live with, knows I can do much more than sunbathe. Todd is extremely smart for a third-grader, and he gives me what I need the most: respect.

Todd and I met about eight months ago, when his family moved from the city to a house in the suburbs. Actually, Todd didn't just meet me. He rescued me from the Bad Place, a pet shop run by a guy named Scarp.

Many humans are prejudiced against reptiles, but Scarp was the worst. "I hate lizards," Scarp used to say. "Just snakes with feet, is all they are." Scarp was a lot nicer to the furry animals than he was to us reptiles. He'd feed the bunnies, puppies, kittens, and hamsters long before he fed us. His favorite pal was a white cat with a bad attitude and plenty of hair. "Look, kitty," Scarp would say, pointing at me. "That lizard's lost his fur! Want him for a snack?" Then the cat would move closer to my cage and show me her needle-sharp teeth. Yikes!

Todd's dad brought him to Scarp's to choose a pet to keep him company, and thank heavens Todd chose me. Scarp said he was glad to be rid of me! Well, I was glad to be rid of him, too.

Todd took me home to the best family a lizard could ever have. He treats me right and so does his big sister, Rae Ann. She's eleven and is always reading books. That's how she found my name, Bima. I'm named for the Sultan of Bima, who discovered the world's largest lizard, a Komodo dragon, in Indonesia. He was a 365-pound porker (the lizard, not the prince). Even though I weigh barely an ounce, I sort of look like him. If you don't believe me, you can find his picture in the *Guinness Book of World Records*.

I love being in the Boucher family. I live in a comfy cage that Dad found in our garage. It used to belong to a mouse. Dad covered the cage walls with screen just for me. It sits on Todd's bedroom floor under a special heat lamp that warms one corner. There's gravel on my cage floor and fresh leaves sprinkled with water for me to sip. Todd feeds me crickets and takes me everywhere with him—into the den to watch TV and even to the dinner table. Of course, I don't eat dull human food that just sits there on the plate. A wiggly, six-legged dinner is more my style.

Todd and I play outside almost every day, so I get plenty of fresh air and sunshine. He knows that's important for a lizard. Todd's also easy to get along with. At least he was, until that morning a few weeks ago when he turned eight.

May 12, Todd's birthday, was circled in red on the calendar in our room. That was the day he got his brand-new black-and-silver Speedster bicycle. It was sitting in the middle of the kitchen when we came out to breakfast. A card tied to the bike's handlebars said, "This is for you to ride in the bike derby. Surprise and Happy Birthday! Love, Mom and Dad."

Todd took one look, grabbed the handle on top of my cage, and ran with me back to our bedroom, yelling, "No thank you! No thank you!" At least he remembered his manners. The ride back to our room was kind of bumpy, so I hung on tight to the cage walls. I wondered what a bike derby was. I also wondered why Todd didn't like his present. I had no clue.

Next thing I heard were slippers scuffing down the hall. They were Mom's. I knew this because I am an expert at recognizing shoe sounds. When you're as dinky as I am, shoes can be dangerous, so you'd better know your shoes. Especially shoes moving in your direction.

Mom came into our room and said, "We thought you'd love a two-wheeler, Todd. With the school bike derby coming up, you'll want—"

"I don't need a bike," Todd interrupted. "I've got my little one with the training wheels."

"You mean that old thing you had at our apartment?" Mom asked. "You've really outgrown it. Besides, don't you want to ride a two-wheeler like your friends?"

"Bima's my friend, and he doesn't ride a bike," Todd said. "Besides, I'm too short for the Speedster."

"That's not true, Todd," said Dad, peeking through the doorway. "We bought you just the right size bike." He knotted his tie as he spoke. "The Speedster is just what you need. Out here, everyone uses bikes. And the school bike derby will be fun. Let's start practicing today after I get home from work."

"Not today," said Todd.

Dad looked very disappointed. Bike riding is just about his favorite thing to do. It is one of the big reasons he wanted to move out to the suburbs—so the family could do more bike riding and outdoor stuff. Every weekend he wears tight black shorts and a bicycle helmet with dark glasses that make him look like an alien insect.

Dad sighed. "I suppose we can wait and go riding this weekend, then—"

"I can't," said Todd, gulping hard like he was going to cry. "I—do I have any more presents?"

Mom looked at Dad. Dad looked at Mom. Neither of them said a word. Rae Ann came in carrying a giant package wrapped in black paper with shiny yellow and purple stars. "Hey! Happy birthday!" she said, handing Todd the package.

"Thanks," he said. He tore off the paper and opened the box. Inside was a genuine G.I. Jim Army Command Center, just like the one Todd and I saw on TV. It had doors and windows that really opened, and little plastic soldiers, jeeps, and trees. "This is so cool," said Todd. "And it's just the right size for Bima!" He looked down at me. "You can be the commander," he promised.

Aw, do I have to? I thought as Todd's hand swooped into my cage to pick me up. This can be scary if you're not used to it—sort of like being plucked up by my one-hundred-million-year-old great uncle Pterodactyl, whose picture is in one of our dinosaur books. The big guys were ferocious, but hey, they're my relatives, and I'm proud of them!

Todd set me on the rug in front of the command post and pushed me gently through its door. There were lots

of green plastic guys in there. They were about my size, but they stood on their hind legs instead of on all fours. I noticed they had guns in their hands, so I scrambled into a corner for cover.

"Oh, Todd. Don't let Bima out of his cage," Mom said. "He'll make a mess."

"No, he won't," Todd said.

No, I won't, I agreed. Would Mom ever understand that lizards are neat and clean? And shedding doesn't count.

Dad said, "Better mind your mother and put Bima back in his cage, Todd. And hurry up, or you'll be late for school."

"Okay, okay," Todd said. In a rush, he grabbed my tail. That startled me so I tried to run away. I felt a jerk and then a teensy ouch like a stubbed toe. I scurried under the command-post table.

"Oh no!" wailed Todd. "Bima's tail broke off!"

"Amazing," said Dad, leaning down to the command-post window and staring at the twitching tail Todd held between his fingers. "It's still moving."

"I hurt him. I'm sorry, Bima. Please don't die," Todd wailed.

I'm not dead, just shorter! Maybe about three inches long now, without that tail . . .

"He's fine," Mom said. "He's under the table. See?

Now put the tail down and go wash your hands. Bima can stay in the command post until after school. He can't get out of there."

That's what you think, Mom.

"You okay, boy?" Todd asked me. He set my ex-tail inside the post.

Rae Ann came over and put her arm around Todd. As usual, she brought the smell of cinnamon with her. Good old Rae Ann. The cinnamon kid. Always chewing on cinnamon-flavored gum or those tiny red-hot candies. She even cleans her teeth with cinnamon dental floss.

"Don't worry," Rae Ann told Todd. "Bima's not hurt. He's magic."

Me, magic?

"He can grow a new tail," Rae Ann explained. "Remember how we read that in the *Encyclopedia of Reptiles?*"

"Oh yeah. I forgot," Todd said.

Big deal, I thought. I wouldn't call growing a new tail magic. It's natural for us lizards. An everyday kind of thing.

"Come on," Rae Ann said. "It's time to get ready for school. You're bringing birthday cupcakes today, right?"

"I'm saving the one with the most frosting for Bima," Todd said. "For after school."

"He won't eat it. He's strictly an insectivore," Rae Ann said.

"Then I'll bring him a cricket," said Todd. "I'll be home soon, boy."

Don't worry about me. I'll be fine. In a few minutes, the family would all be gone to work and school. I'd be alone until 3:00, free to go where I wanted. Free to be me! Good thing Mom didn't know I could escape from the command post.

After they left, I checked my surroundings. That's what a commander does, right? Hey. Those army guys weren't so tough. They were only plastic and couldn't move an inch. Just for fun, I poked one of them over with my snout. Then I saw my tail lying next to him. Ugh.

It doesn't hurt much to lose a tail. I've lost a few. But the first time it happened was a disaster.

When I was a little kid—I mean lizard—I got dropped. It happened at the Bad Place when Scarp was cleaning our cages. He couldn't get his hands on me. "Come here, you," he muttered, grabbing me by the tail. Then he dangled me like one of Mom's drop earrings high above the floor.

It was such a long way down! In a panic, I wriggled. That's when my tail broke. I dropped straight down, just like one of those bungee jumpers you see on the "Extreme Sports" TV show, only I didn't have a cord to stop the fall.

Fortunately, I landed in a box of sawdust, so I didn't get hurt. Just superscared. Normally we lizards love climbing up high onto walls, fences, or tree trunks. Our claws help us grab on with no problem. But ever since Scarp dropped me, I've hated heights. I guess I'm afraid I'll fall again, only this time there won't be any sawdust.

Well, enough of remembering the scary times. That morning in Todd's new army post, I had a day of adventures ahead of me. I crawled out one of the windows and scampered across the carpet. I was alone, uncaged, and ready for action. Where should I go first?

Chapter 2

I had a great day. I decided to sneak a little TV while Mom wasn't there to say no. I found the remote and nosed down hard on the power button. My favorite game show came on. Too bad I wasn't a contestant, since I knew the answer to the big question. It was "How fast can a lizard run?" The answer is eighteen miles per hour, in case you're curious.

"Morning Aerobics with Cindy" was next. I like to keep in shape, so I watched Cindy, who is pretty cute for a human. I kept up until leg lifts. I even tried lifting all four of my legs at once, like an African desert lizard will do when the sand gets too hot. Ooof! I fell flat on my belly. That was plenty of exercise, so I quit.

Later I found a fat cricket behind a log in the fireplace. I played tag with him and then ate him for lunch. In the kitchen I saw a box of protein-shake mix on the table. *Increases Muscle Strength and Energy*, it said in big letters. I wondered if the stuff worked for lizard muscles. I tasted some that had spilled on the floor. Yuck! It needed a few spicy ants to improve the flavor.

You're probably wondering how it is I can read. Allow me to explain. First of all, not all lizards can read. I don't want to brag or anything, but only the most intelligent of us, such as myself, are able to.

I learned by accident. At the pet shop, Scarp kept me in a back corner with no windows. Boring! My fellow reptiles were no help. They'd been there longer than I had, and mostly they slept. But Scarp kept the TV on all day. I could see the screen from my cage. TV became my best (and only) friend.

Every day Scarp turned on "Sesame Street." Not that he liked the show. He hated it, especially when the trash can grouch was on. They were too much alike! But the families who shopped at Scarp's loved "Sesame Street," and he wanted to keep his customers happy. I watched the show every morning. That's where I picked up my first words and learned to tell time.

I really surprised myself when I realized I could read the boxes stacked next to my cage. *Power Kibble,* said one. *Hamster Wheels,* said another. Wow! When I knew I could actually figure out words, I couldn't stop. I read everything I saw, anywhere, anytime. *Kitty Treats! Doggy Softy Pillow—X-Large! Fantastic Fish Fort—Two Aquatic Snails Included!*

Pretty soon I'd read everything in my corner of the shop. I was starved for more, but there was nothing left to read. Then I moved to the Bouchers' house. It was filled with books, magazines, newspapers, labels—a reader's heaven!

At the Bouchers', I read every single day. Todd's birthday morning was no different. I skittered past Rae Ann's room, then skittered back to read the ribbons hanging on her door: *First Place, Sharks Swim Team* and *Runner-Up, All-City Girls' Soccer.* Then I wandered into Mom and Dad's room and spied a bottle of lotion sitting on the lowest bookshelf. The label said, *Softens and moisturizes dry, scaly skin.* Sounded perfect for a lizard, but we kids aren't supposed to touch Mom's things, so I didn't. Instead, I curled up on a sunny patch of carpet and went to sleep.

I woke as the back door opened. *Clackety-clack.* Mom's sandals. Todd and Mom were home!

"I'm hungry," I heard Todd say.

"I'll fix you a snack," Mom said, "while you go check on Bima."

I had to get back to the command post pronto. Otherwise Mom would know I had been out. I tore down the hallway and scooted through the post window.

Todd came in and peeked at me. I'll never get used to how huge humans' faces are, especially when they stare at you from two inches away. Of course, some faces are worse than others. Take Scarp's, for example. Old grumble face. He had eyebrows as big and bumpy as a tree dragon. Yuck!

But Todd's face was smooth and sweet, with a teensy mole on his chin. Today there were also cupcake crumbs on his lower lip. Todd sighed. A strong breeze blew through the command post.

"Hey, Bima, want to go outside and play?" Todd asked. He picked me up and slipped me into his pocket.

Outdoors, Todd set me down under the oak tree so I could run around. Then he grabbed one of the tree's low branches with both hands.

"I'm doing stretches," he said. "To make me taller." He swung his legs back and forth as he hung from the branch.

I hoped Todd's stretches would work. He's the smallest kid in his class. Dad's always saying, "Someone has to be the smallest, and someone has to be the tallest," but Todd just wants to be somewhere in the middle. He tries everything to make himself grow—extra vitamins, food, exercises—but he's still the shortest boy in his grade. Also the youngest. I know just how he feels. It isn't easy being small.

"Hey," someone yelled, scooting over the fence.

Bobby Menlo. *Rhymes with uh-oh.*

Bobby is in Todd's class at school. The kids call him "Mean-lo." He lives nearby, but Todd doesn't like to hang around with him much.

Todd dropped to the ground.

"Wanna play space cops?" Bobby asked. He was wearing his usual baggy jeans, baseball cap, and over-size gray sweatshirt with the sleeves torn off. He grinned wickedly. "Say I capture you."

"Forget it," Todd said. I knew he didn't want to play with Bobby, no matter what the game was.

"I'll let you escape," said Bobby. "Come on."

"Okay," said Todd, giving in to Bobby. Todd put me in his shirt pocket and ran. It was a bouncy ride, so I dove to the bottom of the pocket where I felt safer.

Todd kept going. I peeked out to see where we were. Todd ran to the front porch where his new bike was parked. I heard Bobby following close behind us. "Oh, man, a Speedster!" he said. "It's so cool. When did you get it?"

"This morning, for my birthday," Todd said.

I watched Bobby walk the Speedster around the porch. "Wish I had one of these. The bike derby's pretty soon, and all I have is my dumb brother's old bike—"

"You're supposed to be chasing me," Todd interrupted.

"Let me ride it. Say it's my mega-power rocket. Okay?"

"No," Todd said.

"Then you ride it and chase me."

"No!" Todd said.

"Why not? Don't you *want* to ride it?"

"I just don't feel like it right now," Todd said.

"Aw. Is Toddy scared of the great big bikey?"

"Shut up."

"Make me, shrimp-boy," Bobby answered. He still had one hand on the bike. You could tell he loved touching that Speedster.

"Okay," said Todd. "Watch this."

Uh-oh, Mean-lo!

Todd pushed Bobby's hand away. Bobby laughed and backed down the porch stairs and onto the front walk. "I'm so scared, Toddy. Ha, ha." While Bobby was laughing, Todd released the kickstand. Then he pointed the bike straight at Bobby and shoved it hard. The bike sailed off the porch and onto the walk.

"Here," Todd yelled. "Try riding it now, Mean-lo."

Bobby jumped aside, but the bike caught him on one leg. He fell in the dry grass next to the front walk. The bike clattered to the cement, wheels still spinning.

Bobby got up, covered with little bits of grass, red-faced and limping. "Your bike is stupid! You're stupid!"

He brushed some grass out of his mouth and started crying. "And they don't let babies ride in the derby!" he screamed as he ran off.

Todd moped around the rest of the afternoon. When Dad came home, we were in our bedroom. I was sitting in G.I. Jim's jeep, trying to get the steering wheel to work. Todd was fiddling with some blocks, adding a tower to the army post.

"Hey, birthday boy, how about we practice on the Speedster before dinner?" I guess Dad thought he could get Todd on that bike.

I slipped out of the jeep and into my cage as Todd answered, "I'm too tired. And I have homework."

Dad frowned. "Okay. But remember, you've got to get ready for the derby, right?"

Todd looked away. "I guess," he muttered.

"That's the spirit. Yup, we'll get you set for those races. Show the kids at school how fast that new Speedster really is! I can hardly wait!"

Todd didn't answer. Dad left us. Then Todd smashed his block tower all over the carpet. He didn't clean it up, either.

That night, for Todd's birthday dinner, Mom served his favorite meal—lasagna. Then Rae Ann brought in a birthday cake with eight bright candles. Todd blew out every candle in one big breath. After that, they ate cake and strawberry ice cream, and Todd opened a present from his grandmother. It was a book called *Tons of T-rex: Everything About Your Favorite Dinosaur.* Todd and I were thrilled.

But later, when we were going to sleep, he pounded his pillow with his fist. "What'll I do, Bima? I can't ride a two-wheeler. I never learned when we lived in the city. I can't be in the derby. I'm just a short, dumb baby." Then he cried himself to sleep.

I lay awake in my cage for a long time. The moon shone through our window, lighting up our *Tyrannosaurus rex* poster. The big fella's teeth glimmered, beautiful and sharp. T-rex is not only my ancestor but my personal hero. I would love to be big like him, have those choppers to bite with, those muscles to flex.

But that night I wasn't thinking about bodybuilding—I was worrying about Todd. Ever since he moved here last September, he'd put off learning to ride. Now, with the derby coming up, he was out of time. I had to do something. I knew Cousin Rex would never let a friend down. And I wouldn't either. But how could a snip of a lizard like me help Todd ride a two-wheeler?

Chapter 3

The rest of that week Dad didn't say much about the Speedster. But on Saturday he was determined to get Todd on that bike. "Practice time," he said. He pulled on his special bike-riding gloves.

Todd answered, "No. I can do it myself." As we hurried out the door, he called to Dad, "See? I'm going riding right now. Bima's gonna watch."

Outside, Todd walked the bike down the sidewalk, out of sight of our house. He and I sat on the curb for a while and soaked up some sun. I saw another lizard nearby doing the same thing, but he scurried away before I could introduce myself. Meanwhile, Todd still hadn't gotten on the bike. It seemed like he didn't really plan to practice, after all.

Then Rae Ann showed up, and Todd let her try the Speedster. She sped down the sidewalk and spun a fancy wheelie right in front of us. "Thanks, Todd. Cool bike!" she said, hopping off the Speedster.

"Yeah," said Todd, but he wasn't smiling, and I could tell he felt worse than ever.

On Sunday, Rae Ann went to a friend's. Todd and I built a Lego town and read dinosaur books. Mom and Dad didn't mention the bike all day. I started thinking maybe everyone would just forget about the derby and the Speedster. Maybe Todd's problems would disappear like a fly on a chameleon's tongue!

The next morning, I was dreaming of another wonderful day all to myself when Todd said, "Guess what, Bima? You're going to school with me today."

School? Uh-oh. I remembered school stories the hamster used to tell back at Scarp's—stories about kids squeezing and poking you. I hoped Todd would protect me.

"You'll like my teacher, Mrs. Henley," Todd told me as Dad drove us to school. When we got there, the first thing I noticed about Todd's classroom was that it smelled like paste and old socks. The next thing I noticed was that the room was full of words for me to read. They were everywhere! I saw maps and pictures on the walls with words like *Asia, Africa,* and *South America* beneath them. I saw a bulletin board that said *This Week's Stars* in big yellow letters. I saw shelves stuffed with books near a comfy-looking sofa, and a sign that said *Curl Up and Read*. On the way to Todd's seat, I even read the kids' names that were printed on little signs on their desks: Riggy, Sara, Justin, Shawn, Maria, Tommy, Alex, Erica.

Todd set my cage on the floor next to his desk. Mrs. Henley clapped her hands for silence. "Boys and girls," she said in a whispery voice, "we have a special visitor this morning. Let's focus up front and give Todd our full attention."

Everyone watched as Todd took me out of my cage and walked to the front of the room.

"Todd brought his pet lizard, Bima, for us to meet," Mrs. Henley said.

Todd held me up high and said, "This is Bima, my best friend." Kids started talking and laughing and asking questions all at once. I wished I'd worn earplugs, and I wished I were on the floor.

"Let's use indoor voices so we won't scare Bima," Mrs. Henley suggested.

"But he can't hear us," said one kid. "He doesn't have ears."

This kid obviously knew nothing about lizards.

"Bima hears you," Todd said. "He hears everything."

Way to tell 'em, Todd! He moved me closer to him. That made me feel safer.

Mrs. Henley said, "Todd's right. Lizards do have excellent hearing and vision."

I lifted my head proudly.

"Where are his ears?" asked a girl named Erica. I noticed her ears stuck out a little, and that she wore purple hoop earrings on them.

"Right here." Todd pointed to the flat circles of membrane on the sides of my head.

"Why don't you walk down the rows so everyone can get a closer look at Bima," said Mrs. Henley.

"Wow," said Riggy, a boy with hair like hay. "He must have gotten sunburned. He's peeling."

"He always does that," Todd said. "He's supposed to shed. Little pieces of his skin come off all the time. There's brand-new skin underneath."

Yay, Todd. You are the world's smartest lizard expert.

"Where? Where's the new skin?" someone asked.

"I can't see," someone else complained.

"Can you hold Bima up higher so everyone can see?" Mrs. Henley asked.

Todd lifted me higher.

No! Higher is a bad idea, lady.

I crouched in the center of his open palm and tried not to look down. Memories of the pet-shop fall flashed through my brain. At least Todd wasn't dangling me upside down by my tail!

"What kind of lizard is he, Todd?" Mrs. Henley asked.

A dizzy lizard!

"A Western Fence Lizard. Some people call them bluebellies, because of the pretty bluish-silver color they have on their underside." Todd let them have a peek at my belly. How embarrassing!

"He's like a rainbow," said a girl named Sara.

"Boys and girls, there are more than three thousand different kinds of lizards in the world," Mrs. Henley said.

Even I didn't know that. . . . Mrs. Henley must be pretty smart!

"Wow," said a bunch of kids.

"Wait a minute," said Sara, squinting to see me better. "Where's his tail?"

"It broke off," Todd explained.

Some kids laughed.

"Lizards lose their tails a lot . . ." Todd began. He moved me down closer to him again.

Up, down, up, down. What am I, a flying gecko?

"But it'll only take Bima about a month to grow a new tail," Todd added, finally setting me back in my cage. Phew!

He was right. As long as we are in good health, we can grow a new tail in a snap.

"Who knows what lizards eat?" Mrs. Henley asked.

"Worms!"

"Bugs!"

"Crickets!"

"Sickening!" said Bobby.

Huh! I'd also eat a certain bunch of third-graders, just to keep them quiet. I was exhausted from my guest appearance in Mrs. Henley's class and beginning to feel crabby and tired. I closed my eyes.

"Some lizards eat only vegetables, but Bima eats flies, ants, beetles, and other bugs," said Todd. "I think he needs to rest now," he added.

"You mean he takes naps?" said Bobby. "Like a baby?" And he giggled. Todd glared at him.

"Thank you, Todd." Mrs. Henley pointed to the clock. "It's time for seat work. Everyone to their stations."

I fell asleep. When I woke up, I was starving, so I figured it must be lunchtime. I was right. "You can bring Bima with you to the cafeteria, but keep him in his cage," Mrs. Henley told Todd.

In the cafeteria they were serving tacos. Todd and I sat down, and he began munching his lunch. "You can eat when we get home, okay?" he told me.

But I'm hungry now!

Todd raised his hand to go to the bathroom. "Leave the cage here," said the cafeteria teacher as Todd grabbed the handle. "I'll watch the lizard for you."

"I'll be right back," Todd promised me. The cafeteria teacher stood next to me. Then a kid dropped his plate upside down on the floor, and she ran to help.

I felt safer under my gravel, so that's where I went. A minute later I heard breathing nearby. I peeked out. A face was pressed against my cage. Bobby! "Here, lizard. Here, lizzie, lizzie, lizard," he whispered.

I trembled. Maybe Bobby was still mad at Todd about the Speedster. Maybe he wanted to hurt me and then say it was an accident. I sunk back under the gravel. Then I heard the soft click of my cage door unlatching. No!

"Better leave the lizard alone," said someone else. "Boucher will flip out if he sees you messing with it."

"I was just looking," said Bobby. I peeked out again and was glad to see Bobby move back to his seat. The kids laughed, talked, and ate, except for Erica, whose taco sat uneaten on her tray. Then I spied something delicious, crawling near Erica's plate—a lunch-sized beetle, just for me.

I wanted that beetle. My stomach growled, saying, "Yes! Feed me!" Maybe nobody'd notice if I just nudged open my cage door and—

I slipped out and stalked the bug. I almost had him, but he got away and scurried straight into Erica's taco. I knew I shouldn't crawl into someone's lunch, but I figured Erica wouldn't want a beetle taco, so I dove in after him. Luckily the kids were busy tossing a piece of bread around like a Frisbee, so they still hadn't noticed me.

I crawled farther and farther into the taco darkness, but the beetle had disappeared. I gave up the hunt. But when I tried to turn around and crawl back out, I couldn't move. I was stuck!

Help! I thought. *Save me!* My front foot was trapped in an olive. My back feet couldn't budge. Any second, I could face a horrible death.

Suffocated in salsa.

Buried in refried beans.

I pushed. I clawed. I dug hard with all four feet. Finally, I kicked the olive off and squished and sloshed my way to the light at the end of the taco. I peeked out and—yikes! I was moving off the plate, going up, up toward . . .

Erica's mouth! Her jaws opened wide. She was going to eat me! The silver braces on her front teeth gleamed coldly at me. I jiggled. I wriggled.

"EEEYOO! Something's in my food!" Erica screamed, dropping the taco in her lap and scooting her chair back fast.

Whoa! It was Scarp's all over again. I tumbled out onto Erica's lap and, in a panic, leaped for her arm. My

claws clung fast to her sweater, and she swatted furiously at me. "Help! Get it off me!"

I dodged her hand, dashed down her arm, jumped for the table, and landed *splosh!* right in the middle of Erica's chocolate pudding. Kids were yelling. "Hey! Over there! What's happening?" One boy stood on his table to get a better view. The cafeteria teacher blew her whistle.

Todd came running up. "Stop, stop, you'll hurt him, you'll hurt Bima," he pleaded. He pulled me out of the pudding.

Bobby was laughing so hard that his face was down on his tray. "Boys and girls," said the cafeteria teacher, "return to your seats at once!"

Todd wiped me off with his napkin and put me into my cage, asking over and over, "Bima, are you all right?"

Barely. I'm sticky all over, and I smell like a candy bar!

Bobby was still giggling. But then someone came up behind him and put her hands on his shaking shoulders. "What on earth is happening here?" Mrs. Henley asked.

Chapter 4

Back in the classroom, Mrs. Henley steered Bobby to a seat near her desk. "No one, I repeat, *no one* is to disturb Bima again." She frowned worriedly at me. "What happened in the cafeteria was a result of bad decisions," she told the class.

Everyone looked at Bobby, who fiddled with his pencil. "Anyone who was a part of that crowd in the cafeteria was participating in something unkind and dangerous," said Mrs. Henley. "This afternoon I want each of you to write about how you could have made better choices. And Bobby, I'll need you to stay in at the next recess."

"All I did was unlatch the cage door—" Bobby began.

"Do we have to write even if we weren't the one that put Bima in the taco?" Riggy asked.

"Even if you weren't the one," said Mrs. Henley. "I think I saw just about everyone in our class laughing at Erica during lunch."

"Thanks a lot, Bobby," someone said.

"I never touched that lizard," said Bobby.

"Yeah, sure," said someone else. Bobby put his head down on his desk. Everyone was blaming him for what had happened. It didn't seem right.

Hey, guys! I wanted to say. *Bobby didn't put me in the taco. I put myself in there.*

After the kids finished writing and came back from afternoon recess, Mrs. Henley wrote two huge words on the blackboard:

BIKE DERBY

Two words I didn't want to read. I watched Todd. His right foot was jiggling, the way it does when he's upset.

"Before we go home today, we need to talk about what is happening next Saturday, May twenty-fourth," said Mrs. Henley. "Have you all marked your calendars?"

"Yes, yes," a trillion voices answered. After that, everyone was buzzing about the derby except for Todd. He slumped down into his chair as if he wanted to disappear.

"Mrs. Henley, Mrs. Henley," a bunch of kids called. "Can we—" "Do we—" "When is—" "How do you—"

Their teacher laughed. I liked that. Her laugh reminded me of the wind chimes that clink on the Bouchers' back porch. "One at a time, please," she said.

"Only five more days till the derby," Erica said.

"Correct. Who can tell us what happens on Derby Day?"

Riggy raised his hand. "Everyone rides in races and stuff . . . then there's a parade—"

"Not everyone," Bobby interrupted. "Just third-through sixth-graders. Not the—" He turned to gaze straight at Todd. "—baby kids," he finished. Someone snickered. Todd stared down at his desk.

"Are we allowed to decorate our bikes for the parade?" asked a girl who sat in back. She wore glasses with blue-speckled frames that reminded me of a robin's egg that Todd and I found once in the backyard.

"Yes, if you like," said the teacher. "Boys and girls, before we get ready to go home, you may sign up for derby events. The lists are on the back counter."

Some kids put away papers and packed backpacks while others, including Todd and me, went to check the sign-up sheets.

"Mrs. Henley," Sara called, waving her hand like a windshield wiper. "Can anyone sign up for any events they want?"

"Anyone but Todd," Bobby answered. "He can't even ride—"

"You may be in as many and whatever events you choose except for trick riding, of course. That's just for the sixth-graders," Mrs. Henley said as she walked over to Bobby and put one hand firmly on his shoulder.

That shut him up for a minute, but as soon as the teacher was out of hearing range, Bobby turned to Erica. "Watch out, there's Todd's ferocious lizard! He's coming this way! Careful, everybody, Erica's afraid of lizards."

"Actually," said Erica, sniffing with disdain, "I am only slightly herpetophobic."

"Slightly *what?*" asked Riggy as he grabbed a pencil out of Bobby's hand.

"Herpetophobic, reptilophobic, whatever," said Erica. "Afraid of lizards. And I certainly don't like them for lunch."

Thank goodness for that!

"Phobias are extremely common," Erica continued. "For example, acrophobia, a fear of heights, is a problem for lots of people."

And even some lizards, I thought miserably.

"How do you know so much about it?" Bobby asked.

"My mom is a psychologist," Erica said. "She told me about phobias. There are some really weird ones, like ichthyophobia, the fear of fish, and myxophobia, the fear of—"

"Electric mixers?" Riggy asked. Everyone laughed.

"No, fear of *slime*," said Erica.

"Hey, everybody!" Bobby interrupted. "Todd can't be in the derby because he has bikeophobia!"

"Liar," muttered Todd.

"Ooooo, Boucher," said a bunch of kids.

I was so mad at Bobby I wanted to flatten him. I wished I was a horny toad so I could squirt blood on him. I wished I was a Gila monster so I could spit poison on him. But even though I wished hard, I was still an ordinary lizard, stuck in my cage.

"Mean-lo, you don't know anything," Todd said. "See? I'm signing up right now"—he checked the top of the sheet—"for the obstacle course."

I felt sick. *The obstacle course? No, Todd, no! What about the obstacle of not knowing how to ride your bike?*

Meanwhile, Mrs. Henley came over to the crowd that had gathered. "Let's continue this discussion another day," she said. "Your homework is written on the board. Everyone back to their seats."

"Hey," said Bobby, returning to his desk. "I've got homeworkophobia!"

"Yeah, me too!" Riggy said.

"Which row is ready to go home?" asked the teacher.

In two seconds every kid was sitting up straight and absolutely quiet.

Over here, Mrs. Henley. I'm ready to go home, yes, I'm ready, ready, ready!

After we were excused, Todd and I went to the parking lot to wait for Mom. He took me out and set me on his shoulder. I crawled under his collar so I wouldn't have to see how far off the ground I was.

Bobby came up and poked Todd's shoulder. "Hey," he said. "Isn't your name Baby Boucher, the famous bikeophobic? Or is it Tiny Toddy?" Poke, poke.

Okay, I thought. Enough. I pretended I was my Cousin Rex and then viciously chomped down on Bobby's finger. Yeechh! He tasted terrible. But it was worth it. I can't bite hard enough to draw blood, but I scared him.

"Hey!" Bobby howled. "Your stupid lizard bit me!"

"Stay out of his way, then," Todd said. "You practically killed him when you put him in Erica's taco!"

"I told you, I never touched him. I wouldn't want to. He's gross!"

Now hold on, here. . . .

"You were trying to hurt him, and you know it," said Todd.

Bobby scuttled away, holding his bitten finger. "I'll probably catch rabies," he yelled.

"Definitely hydrophobophobic," said Erica, who was standing nearby.

Bobby looked at her, then back at Todd. "You're gonna get it, Boucher."

Chapter 5

At dinner that night, Dad asked, "So how was Bima's visit to school?"

Todd took a bite of bread. "Okay, except Mean-lo put Bima in Erica's taco, and everybody got in trouble."

No, I put me in Erica's taco. . . .

"That's awful! What a cruel thing to do to poor Bima!" Mom said.

"Bobby seems to enjoy causing trouble," Dad said.

"Yeah," Todd agreed. "Then Bima fell in the chocolate pudding, but I rescued him. He's all right now."

"Wow," said Rae Ann. "A chocolate lizard."

"It wasn't funny," said Todd.

It sure wasn't!

"Sorry. I was just kidding," said Rae Ann. She helped herself to more macaroni and cheese, then asked, "Mom, could I borrow your sewing basket?"

"What for?"

"The derby. Carly and I are decorating our bikes."

"Sounds like fun," Mom said. "Doesn't it, Todd?"

"No," Todd said, stuffing his mouth full of macaroni.

He doesn't need decorations. He needs bike-riding lessons, fast.

"Mom," Rae Ann said, putting down her fork. "Todd can't be in the derby. He doesn't know how to ride yet."

"But he's been practicing, haven't you, son?" asked Dad.

"Uh . . . sure," Todd said. "Maybe I'll even ride the . . . the obstacle course."

Rae Ann's big brown eyes got bigger. "Obstacle course? Are you crazy? That's the hardest event there is, except for the sixth-graders' trick riding."

"I don't care," Todd said.

Everything got really quiet after that. Then Mom said, "I'm sure Todd will do just fine at the derby. Now, who wants dessert?"

After dinner, Todd stretched out on the living-room floor to do his math homework. Rae Ann settled next to him and opened a magazine. While Dad read the paper, Mom looked through her sewing basket for things to give Rae Ann.

I pressed my snout against the cage wall, trying to read Rae Ann's magazine. Rae Ann saw me. "Bima wants to read with me," she said. "Can't we let him out?"

Dad chuckled. "I doubt if the lizard wants to read, Rae Ann. . . ."

"He does, too," muttered Todd.

"He's incredibly smart," Rae Ann said. "Please?"

Mom and Dad looked at each other. "I suppose it's okay," Mom said. "But keep an eye on him."

"All *right!*" said Todd, cheering up. Rae Ann opened my cage door. I stepped out and strolled onto the magazine for a closer look. The story was called "Skating Sharp with Roller Racers."

"Mom, I really need some Rollerblades. Then I could practice with the boys' roller-hockey team," Rae Ann said.

"Sounds dangerous," said Mom.

"Yeah," said Todd.

"Oh, Mom," said Rae Ann.

"The bike derby isn't even over and you're rushing into the next thing," Mom added. "Maybe you should slow down a bit and finish these decorations. Here. I found sequins and ribbon for you to use." She handed Rae Ann a tangle of things from her basket.

Rae Ann began gluing shiny little dots to a triangle of blue paper. I kept reading, and Todd kept doing his math. But Rae Ann couldn't sit still. She stopped gluing and pointed to the magazine, saying "Dad. These are the exact skates I want."

"Hmm," said Dad, peering at the magazine. "This hockey stuff does look too rough."

"It just looks that way in the picture."

"How do you know?" Todd asked. "You've never even played it before."

"But I know I could do it," said Rae Ann, going back to her gluing, and I believed her. Things come easily for Rae Ann. She's always trying something new. I'll bet if she were turned into a lizard, she'd catch the fastest, juiciest fly on her first try!

"These word problems are too hard," Todd complained.

Words? Did someone say words? Allow me to assist!

"Let's see," said Rae Ann. I moved over so I could read Todd's problem, too. It asked, "How many hours until . . ." Hmm . . . I wondered how many hours there were until the derby. Let's see, the living-room clock said 8:00. The derby was this Saturday at 9:00 A.M. Phew! Too much math for me! But however many hours Todd had left, I knew they weren't enough.

After they finished Todd's math problem, Rae Ann held up her flag and said, "Here it is. What do you think?"

I liked it. Some of the sequins spilled onto our magazine. They were as shiny as scrumptious little ladybugs.

"Want a flag for your bike, too?" Rae Ann asked Todd.

"No, thank you," said Todd, sinking so low his nose practically touched his math paper.

"Okay, but if you change your mind—"

"*Ooooh. Oh. Owww!*" Suddenly Todd dropped his pencil and doubled over in the shape of a paper clip.

"What's wrong?" Dad asked, rushing over to him.

"My stomach," Todd groaned. "*Owww!*"

"You were okay a minute ago," Rae Ann said.

"Maybe I have heatstroke." Todd moaned and crossed his arms tight over his middle.

"Just because the weather's warm doesn't mean you have heatstroke," Mom said. "Maybe you ate too much macaroni. You'd better go lie down. Rae Ann, put Bima back in his cage and take him to Todd's room."

"Come on, partner," Dad said, half leading, half carrying Todd down the hall. Rae Ann set my cage down and left our bedroom. Dad stayed to tuck us in and said, "As soon as you're feeling better, we'll go on a long bike ride to town, just the two of us. How about it?"

Todd just groaned.

Later, after Dad left our bedroom, Todd snapped on the light, took me out of my cage, and put me on his pillow. "Don't worry, pal," he told me. "I'm not really sick."

Hmmm.

"I'm just rehearsing for Saturday. If I'm sick, I won't

have to go to the derby. Actually, just thinking about the derby makes me feel sick," he added.

I'll bet it does.

"So I'm not exactly lying."

I shook my head no to make him feel better.

"Lying about what?" someone asked. Someone who smelled like cinnamon. Rae Ann's tongue was bright red from chewing on her candy.

"Uh, nothing," Todd mumbled weakly. "What do you want?"

"I just came in to say good night. You're gonna pretend to be sick on Derby Day, aren't you?" Rae Ann popped more red hots in her mouth and chewed harder. "Well, forget it," she said. "You'll have to learn to ride the bike sooner or later. We live in the suburbs now. Everyone has a bike. You've got to get with the program, Todds. Besides, if you faked being sick again, nobody would believe you anyway."

"I don't care," Todd said. "I'll get well and then I'll have a . . . a . . ."

"Relapse," Rae Ann said. "It won't work. You can't stay sick forever. Just learn to ride the Speedster. It isn't that hard."

"Maybe not for you. But I'm so short my feet won't even reach the pedals."

I know just how you feel, pal!

"You've grown some this year."

Right, Rae Ann!

"No, I haven't. I never grow," insisted Todd, turning his face to the wall. "Bobby is just as much bigger than me as he was last fall."

"That's because he's growing, too," Rae Ann explained. "You'll never catch up to a hulk of a kid like Bobby. And I'm sure Mom and Dad picked out a bike just the right size for you."

Listen to your sister, will ya?

"You're just saying that," Todd said. "The Speedster is huge compared to my old bike." He stroked the top of my head. It felt great. Now, if he could just scratch down a little farther on my back . . . "Hey," Todd said. "Did you know Bima can shut his eyelids up instead of down?"

Now this was getting interesting. I'd never paid much attention to my eyelids.

"Stop changing the subject," Rae Ann said.

"I just want you to look at Bima," said Todd.

Rae Ann sighed. "Oh, all right." She leaned down close to me. Her eyes stared into mine. I could see my reflection in them. I gave her a little wink.

"Wow," she said. "I could swear that lizard just winked at me. His eyes are beautiful. Black, with sparkly gold around the middle . . ."

"Lights out," Mom called from the living room.

"Okay," Rae Ann called back. She patted Todd's arm. "Don't worry about the derby. We'll think of something."

"Okay," Todd said, slipping me into my cage.

" 'Night, Todds," Rae Ann said. " 'Night, Bima."

Todd sank back on the pillow and looked up. I looked up, too, and saw the glow-in-the-dark stars Rae Ann had stuck on our ceiling for us. I love those stars. They look like the real thing! Todd yawned, then turned over. That was when I noticed that he had left my cage door unlatched again.

An hour later, all was quiet except for the tick-tock of the big clock in the hall. It had been so hot that day that the house was as warm as a sunny afternoon. I was bone-tired from my day at school and soon fell asleep.

It seemed only a few minutes later when I woke up. But the clock struck 5:00. Almost morning. I was turning over in my gravel for a little more sleep when I heard a strange sound sailing through the open window. *Clickety-click. Spinnity-clickety-click.*

Bike wheels were spinning. But whose?

Chapter 6

I shook myself. I decided I must have been having a bike-derby nightmare, hearing the spin of wheels in my sleep. . . . *Clickety-click.* That sound again! This was no dream.

It was coming from our backyard. What was going on? I had to know. We lizards are territorial, and the Bouchers' backyard is my territory.

First, I checked Todd. He was snoring softly. Then I light-footed it out of the bedroom and down the hall to the back door. *Clickety-spinnity-click.* There it was again!

I squeezed under the screen door and onto the back porch. Dawn was barely pinking the sky, but I could see enough. It was the Speedster wheels clicking. Someone was riding it—someone dressed in . . . a giant sweatshirt and baggy pants. Bobby!

I melted into the dark corner of the porch. Bobby was probably still mad about my biting him, and I wasn't taking any chances on being seen.

Bobby rode the Speedster in slow, small circles on the

patio. Around and around he rode, humming, going nowhere. He seemed to be in another world. Then he stopped, got off, and slowly ran his hand along the fender and the handlebars. I wished he were as nice to me as he was to the Speedster!

Bobby glanced at the paling sky, then parked the bike exactly where Todd had left it last. He even threw Todd's T-rex shirt over the seat where Todd had left it yesterday afternoon. Then he scrambled over the back fence.

Wow. Bobby must have really loved that bike to sneak into our yard in the dark just to steal a ride. I hoped that was all he planned on stealing.

I figured as long as I was outside I might as well hunt a little breakfast before the Bouchers got up. I skittered off the porch and onto the lawn. The sky glowed with new light, and the grass sang with crickets. I caught a couple and munched them while blades of grass tickled my toes.

After a few minutes, full and sleepy, I headed for the house. But suddenly a shadow swallowed the dawn. I heard the warning sound that every small creature learns to fear: wings whirring above me. The wings of a feathered hunter.

It was a small hawk. He circled lower, lower, preparing to snatch me in his talons.

I ran for my life. I should have stayed inside! I kept thinking of "The Law of the Jungle," a TV show about big animals devouring smaller ones. I ran harder, trying to reach some bushes or a rock to hide under. The thick, warm air felt as if it were wrapping around me, holding me back. My feet slipped on the grass, and the backyard blurred past as I searched for shelter. "Scrawww!" screeched the hawk.

Then those brawny wings blew a breeze right down my back as the bird swooped between me and the bushes. Where could I go? I charged back to the patio and nearly ran into the Speedster. Panic pushed me up the wheel and onto the fender. I dove into the sleeve of Todd's forgotten shirt, shook all over with fear, gasped for air, and waited, waited, waited. Silence. Then another "Scrawww!" from farther away.

I waited a long time before I peeked out. The hawk had disappeared. I'd escaped. I was okay. Time to go back to my bedroom and to Todd, who would be waking up soon.

Then I remembered where I was. I looked down.

Below me, over the edge of the bike seat, was nothing but empty air. I'd climbed up there so fast, I hadn't noticed how high off the ground I was. My leg muscles went mushy with fear. I thought of Scarp and my long-ago fall in the pet shop.

I turned away from the seat's edge, huddled back inside the shirt, and closed my eyes. I was the world's worst coward, afraid of heights, an acrophobic. I shamed the reputation of high-climbing reptiles. I was a disgrace to all lizardom.

I dreamed I was the prisoner of a giant spider. It had a face like Scarp's, and a sharp beak that opened and said, "Scrawww! Scrawww!" Its sticky web twined tight around my legs. Hot breath blew from its mouth. From behind the spider, a speedy gecko that smelled like cinnamon popped up and chattered, "It's easy! Easy!"

Then a familiar voice ended my nightmare. "He's gone," Todd wailed. "I can't find him anywhere."

I opened my eyes. I'd fallen asleep inside the T-shirt on the bike seat. My toes were tangled in some threads. As I wiggled loose and crawled into the daylight, I heard Dad call from his car in the driveway, "Don't worry, son. We can get another lizard."

"No! I only want Bima!" Todd shouted from his bedroom window.

That's right, kid. I'm one of a kind.

"You and Rae Ann go ahead," I heard Mom say to Dad. "I'll drive Todd to school later."

"Bima! Here, boy. Come out, now. Bima!" Todd said as he moved through the house.

I crouched on top of the shirt and waited. Then I heard Mom and Todd talking in the kitchen. "Did you look under the gravel in his cage?" she asked. "What about his favorite sun spots?"

"How do you know about those?" Todd asked sadly.

"I know what lizards like," Mom answered. "I know they need their sunshine."

Right, Mom! And I also need Todd to get me off this bike!

"I searched the whole house," Todd said between sobs, "and he's gone, Mom. I'll never see him again!"

"Calm down," Mom said. "I'll help you find him. He's got to be around here somewhere. Go look under the sofa."

"I tried there already!" cried Todd.

"Try again," said Mom. "Or maybe he's in the living-room plants. I'll just check here in the kitchen."

I could see Mom through the screen door. She glanced outside. *Here! I'm over here!*

"He's not in the plants," yelled Todd. "He's not anywhere!"

"We'll find him," called Mom. "You left your shirt outside again, Todd," she added, pushing open the door and walking over to the bike. *Yes!* As she came closer, I did a lizard push-up, lifting my chin high in the air, then dipping it down to my toes. I do them all the time to increase my muscle power.

I did three more.

It worked. Mom saw me. "Oh, my goodness!" she said. "Look, Todd, look here! I found him, right on your T-shirt! I found Bima!"

Todd came running outside, scooped me up, and then held me against his chest. "I knew you wouldn't run away and leave me. See, Mom? He was on my bike the whole time."

"What I want to know is, how did he get outside?" Mom asked.

"I don't know," Todd said. "But I bet he just wanted some exercise. Didn't you, boy?"

I nodded.

"But why on earth would he climb onto your bike?" Mom asked.

To escape being breakfast, of course!

"Maybe he likes my T-rex shirt. They're related, you know. Or maybe . . . maybe he wanted to take a bike ride." Todd put me in his shirt pocket, sat on the Speedster, and seemed to be thinking over what he'd just said. "Is that what you wanted?" he asked me. "A little ride?"

I could hardly believe it. I moved my head up and

down like Rae Ann's yo-yo. I'd do whatever it took to keep Todd interested in the bike.

"Yeah," Todd whispered. "Just a little ride." He flipped the kickstand up and scooted the bike along with his feet. Mom just watched us. She didn't say a word. I think she was as shocked as I was, seeing Todd on the Speedster.

We rolled slowly around the patio. He kept saying, "Okay, Bima, okay, here we go, whoa, hold on!" and things like that.

I held on, all right. How I longed for my cage, safe and solid on the bedroom floor! I'd been high off the ground for so long I might sprout wings soon.

But I knew this was important, so I rode in his pocket and tried not to look down.

Todd kept scooting and wobbling, scooting and wobbling. "It's hard to keep my balance," he said. "But let's try again, okay?"

Mom watched a while longer and then went in the house. A little while later she drove Todd to school. When she got back, she came into my bedroom. "How would you like a nice sunbath on the kitchen floor?" Wow! I did a happy push-up to let her know it was a good idea.

Gently she lifted me out of my cage and carried me

to the warmest spot on the kitchen floor tiles, right by the big window where the sun pours in. She touched my head with her fingertip. "You are an even better friend to Todd than I realized," she said. "You know what's going on, don't you?"

I nodded.

"Good heavens, I'm talking to a lizard," she said. "And he's answering!"

Later, when I poked around in the house plants, she didn't seem to mind at all. "Good boy," she said. "Catch a few spiders while you're in there." Mom needed me to help her! So I did. Yes siree, I was really a part of the family now.

The next day after school, Todd's practicing was the same, except now we were scooting along the front walk. I was riding pretty high, so mostly I hid deep inside the pocket to keep my acrophobia under control.

On the third afternoon, he said, "Okay, I'm ready. Let's try pedaling." He pushed off hard, then jammed his feet onto the pedals. He rolled for a few sidewalk squares and then braked. He'd done it. He'd balanced the two-wheeler for five whole seconds on his own.

From there it was a slow but steady start-and-stop, each time a little longer, until we were riding along the sidewalk at a pretty good speed. Down the street we breezed, past one, two, three houses.

"Hey," breathed Todd. "This is like flying. We're doing it. We're really doing it."

And we were. We practiced the rest of the week, and Todd improved. When Rae Ann got home, she'd come out and give Todd directions like "Keep those pedals moving!" and "Don't look down, look ahead!" And when Dad drove home from work and saw Todd riding for the first time, he was so surprised that he almost crashed the car into the garage door.

Even though the bike almost fell a couple of times, Todd stopped it by putting his foot on the sidewalk. It was a bumpy ride, but we got no bruises. Each day before dinner, Dad and Rae Ann and Mom all came outside to watch and cheer. "Way to go, Todd," Dad said.

On Friday afternoon, Todd ran into the bedroom. "Come on, Bima. The derby's tomorrow, and we've got to practice for the obstacle course."

I was so glad Todd was riding his bike now, I think I would have said yes to anything. Then I saw what he'd done.

Todd had stacked cardboard boxes into tall, shaky towers. He'd made a zigzaggy trail of them all the way down the sidewalk. Lots of lurches ahead. Lots of sharp turns, too. *Couldn't I just stay in my cage and watch?* I wondered.

All of a sudden we took off. "We're rolling now, good buddy," Todd said. He got that line from a driver on the "Monster Truck Show." He steered his bike around the first tower. "That was tight," he said.

No kidding!

"Whoa! Don't know if I can—"

Todd jerked the wheel too hard and threw the Speedster off balance. I saw it coming. There was nothing to do but squeeze my eyes shut tight. Ooof! We toppled over onto the grass next to the walk. Fortunately for me, Todd fell on his backside.

"Man! Those turns are tough," Todd said, getting up and brushing himself off. After he made sure I was okay, Todd got up and walked the bike to the beginning of the course. He wasn't quitting. I squeezed my eyes shut again.

Then Rae Ann came streaking toward us, riding her bike with no hands. "Bima looks a little scared," she said, skidding to a neat stop.

A little?

"Here, I'll take him inside for you."

Good thinking, Rae Ann!

She tried to pluck me out of Todd's pocket, but he stopped her.

"Leave him alone. He likes riding, don't you, pal?"

I hissed, but Todd didn't seem to notice. We took off again before Rae Ann could reach me. I sank into the pocket and hoped our practice would end soon.

I heard the *crickle-crackle* of plastic and knew that Rae Ann was opening a new bag of red hots. "Wait a minute," she called. "You need more obstacles than this. And your path needs to be twistier." I peeked out just as she began rearranging Todd's box towers.

"Hey! Leave my stuff there!" Todd yelled.

"But, Todd, how do you expect to win if—"

"I don't want to win," Todd said. "I just want to ride." He straddled the bike and planted himself in front of Rae Ann, blocking her way.

Way to defend your territory, kid!

"Okay, okay," said Rae Ann, backing off. "I'll just watch, I promise."

Todd took off again. We rode around those boxes all afternoon, with Rae Ann shouting, "That's the way, Todd, keep going!" My insides felt like scrambled eggs. Thank goodness the derby was tomorrow, and I could stay home and take a sunbath like a lizard should.

That night at dinner, Todd said, "Bima and I are gonna be in the derby. We're gonna try to win the obstacle course."

Wait a minute, here. We are not in the derby. You are in the derby.

"Now, son," Dad said, "Bima can't go to the derby. It would be a dangerous place for a loose lizard."

Good point, Dad.

"Anyway," Rae Ann asked, "what do you need Bima for?"

Yeah. What do you need me for?

"He's my lucky lizard," Todd said. "Like your rabbit's foot, Rae Ann. When Bima's with me, I can ride my Speedster."

I've always said I was a lucky guy—I mean, lizard. But not that kind of lucky. . . .

"Listen, Todd, good-luck charms are just pretend," Rae Ann said.

Correct.

"Bima is not pretend," Todd said.

"I didn't mean—"

"The lizard is not going to the derby," Mom said, "and that's final."

Todd stood up fast. His chair clattered to the floor. "But I can't ride without him. I can't!"

"Of course you can," Dad said. "Now, sit down." He gave Todd a no-funny-business look.

Todd picked up the chair and sat. But he didn't say another word, not even when Mom asked if he wanted some caramel frozen yogurt for dessert.

I, on the other hand, thought yogurt sounded like a

super idea. Perhaps with a bit of crunchy centipede sprinkled on top? I felt like celebrating. No bike derby for me. No siree.

Later that night, when we were going to sleep, Todd whispered, "Don't worry, Bima. I know you want to ride with me in the derby. I'll get you there all right. I'll just smuggle you in my pocket. Nobody will notice."

No, no. I want to stay home!

"I'm sure glad you'll be there with me. 'Night, Bima."

When I closed my eyes, I saw bike wheels racing toward me. I saw kids chasing around, paying no attention to where their shoes landed. I saw a swervy, curvy obstacle course. Finally, I fell into an exhausted sleep.

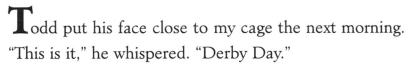

Chapter 8

Todd put his face close to my cage the next morning. "This is it," he whispered. "Derby Day."

I tried hard to be unfriendly. I hissed. I wished I had a nasty blue tongue to flick like my Australian cousin does. When Todd stuck his hand in my cage, I snapped at him. I'd had enough.

"Hey, stop that," he said. "Don't you understand? You have to go with me so I can ride. Please." He looked so worried that I gave up my dream of staying home and reluctantly hopped onto his hand.

"There," he said. He slipped me into his shirt pocket. *Ow!* It had a Velcro closing. That stuff scratches my skin like sandpaper. It figured. What could I expect on this Day of Certain Disaster? I curled up in the lint and stale cracker crumbs at the bottom of the pocket. I tried meditating, the way they do on the "Say Yes to Yoga" show, but I was too nervous.

So was Todd. I could tell, because we made three trips to the bathroom before Dad put the bikes on the bike rack and drove us all to school. On the way, I peeked out of the pocket. We were in the backseat, so I decided it was safe for me to look out the window and read traffic signs. But after "Caution!" "Curves ahead!" and "Stop!" I gave up and sank back into Todd's pocket.

"Have fun," Dad said, stopping the car a few minutes later. I guessed we were at the school now. "Wear your helmets, ride carefully . . . and Todd . . . I think you'd better steer clear of Bobby."

"That's too many things to remember!" Todd said.

I knew Dad didn't trust Bobby. I thought about Bobby's early-morning ride on the Speedster. Too bad I couldn't talk with Dad about it.

"Mom and I will be back later to watch you and Rae Ann," said Dad. The car door opened, and Todd climbed out. I heard Dad take the bikes off the rack. Then a door slammed, and the car left.

"This is your big day," I heard Rae Ann say. She was so close, I could hear her chomping on some gum. "Good luck, Todds," she said.

Todd answered, "With Bima I always have good luck."

Oops.

"What do you mean, 'with Bima'?"

At the sound of my name, I peeked out of the pocket. Todd looked down at me. So did Rae Ann.

"You shouldn't have brought him here," said Rae Ann. "You don't need him to help you ride."

"But Bima's magic," Todd said. "You even told me so. And he loves riding with me on the Speedster."

"Oh, Todd. All right, but keep Bima in your pocket." She patted his shoulder. "I'll be cheering for you!" She left to find her friends.

As soon as she was gone, Todd wheeled the Speedster over to the edge of the parking lot. Then he lifted me out of his pocket and held me in the palm of his hand. "Look, Bima, there's Mr. Pinker, our school principal."

Pinker wore dark glasses, and his bald head shone in the bright May sunshine. He smeared some lotion on top of his head and then tapped the microphone with his finger. It crackled with static. "If everyone will move clear of the course"—he waved his hand at the field, where a flurry of flags and balloons flew in the breeze—"we can start. Let the bike derby begin!"

Pinker pushed his glasses up on his beak nose. " 'Stop and Go' is our first event," he announced.

Todd sat on the grass with me still in his hand. From there we could see the list of events on the sign next to Pinker. After "Stop and Go" were lots of different races. Then they had a relay, a dirt-bike race, and finally the obstacle course. After that were the sixth-grade trick riders, and last would be the victory parade.

We watched the kids in "Stop and Go." They had to start riding, then stop when the whistle blew. The kid who stopped first and cleanest the most times won. That was Bobby. Even on his brother's rusty old bike, he was a terrific rider. But when he passed us, I dove into the pocket. I still wasn't sure what he'd do if he saw me.

After that we watched a bunch of straight-ahead races. Erica tied with a fourth-grade girl in one of those. Rae Ann won second place in a race with other older kids. Then came a relay race with mixed teams of kids from third through sixth grades. Bobby was on a team with older kids, and he helped them win. But as he charged over the finish line, his bike made a terrible racket that reminded me of Godzilla clearing his throat. The back fender fell off, and the bike's chain dangled loosely in the dirt.

"Hey, Menlo," someone called from the crowd. "Looks like you need a new bike!" Bobby dragged what was left of his bike off the field. He didn't even stay to get his team's first-place ribbon.

"The dirt bikers are next, then it's our turn," said Todd. The dirt bikers had to ride over bumps and rocks and holes. This time, a fifth-grader named Aaron won. When Pinker handed him his blue ribbon, the kid smiled. He was covered in dust. Even his teeth were dusty.

"We would have messed up on that event," said Todd.

I know, I know!

"The obstacle course will complete this portion of the derby," boomed Pinker. "It is a difficult ride and requires excellent balance."

And definitely does not require lizards!

"Obstacles. That's us, boy. Wow, this is pretty scary. . . ."

Sure is!

"Let's sit on the grass until our turn," Todd said. He was sweating and biting his fingernails, too.

The obstacle-course riders went one at a time. First up was Riggy. "Good luck to all of you," Pinker said before giving the signal for Riggy to start.

Good luck. There were those words again. I hated being Todd's good-luck charm. He would probably take me on his bike for years, and then, when he was older, I'd have to ride with him on a skateboard, and if I lived to be a very old lizard, I'd have to help him learn to drive a car, or even a big rig! The worst part was, Todd didn't really need me with him. Instead, he needed to count on himself to do the things he wanted to do.

We watched Riggy's bike tires zip around boxes and cones. He knocked a couple over and finished with a pretty good score.

More riders took their turn. Todd and I moved to the edge of the path to get a better view. Rae Ann had been right—the course was much harder than we'd thought. A couple of kids fell in the middle and were disqualified. They walked their bikes off the course. Then a girl named Megan swerved on the skinniest part of the course and fell hard. Her dad helped her up. Her legs were scraped, and her nose was bleeding. "Wow," Todd said.

"Todd Boucher is our last rider," Pinker announced as some helpers replaced the knocked-over cones and boxes.

"Here we go," he told me, setting me on the grass while he retied his shoelaces and put on his helmet.

That's when I decided. There was only one way I could make Todd count on himself to ride in the derby—I would leave him alone. He'd have to ride without me. It would be scary for me to run loose on the playground, but it was my last chance to really, truly help my friend.

So while Todd was busy fastening the strap on his helmet, I took off. I ran through the soft, spongy grass, careful to avoid bike tires and wandering shoes. Feeling like Super Lizard, I darted far away from the course and toward the shelter of a picnic table.

"Todd Boucher," boomed the microphone. "Please come to the starting line." I turned around and saw Todd on his hands and knees, searching the grass, then checking his pockets over and over. I knew who he was looking for.

Go, Todd. Forget about finding me. It's your turn. Take it!

Finally Todd walked the Speedster to the start line.

"Ready?" Pinker asked.

Todd stood staring at the course ahead of him. His fists were tight on the handlebars. He didn't move.

Chapter 9

I watched from the shade of the table. Pinker leaned over the microphone once again. "Let's go," he told Todd.

"Wait," Todd said. He searched his pocket again. Some kids laughed.

"Quit stalling," someone yelled.

"He can't ride that bike," Bobby shouted.

Thanks a lot, Mean-lo. Thanks for embarrassing Todd in front of the whole school.

"It's now or never," Pinker said.

Todd straightened up. "I—I'm ready," he called to Pinker.

That's it, pal. Go for it!

The principal lifted his arm in the air. "On your mark, get set, *go!*" he yelled. Todd took off.

He steered around the first cones with no problem.

Someone cheered, and someone else called, "Careful now. You're on a two-wheeler."

Todd kept pedaling quickly, steering, and watching the course.

Yay, Todd! I thought, but I knew it wasn't over yet. The course got harder. On the skinny part of the path, the bike's front wheel wobbled as Todd turned tightly around a pile of boxes. He knocked them over.

Uh-oh. Pedal faster, pal. Faster.

As if he heard me, Todd's feet pumped harder. The bike righted itself and sailed neatly around the next cone and headed for the big curve.

Someone clapped.

Another curve. Another wild wobble. Two cones down, and Todd zigzagging like crazy! Then came a big dip. He hit it hard, and the bike skidded in the soft dirt, going slower and slower.

Don't stop. Whatever you do, don't stop, I thought as hard as I could.

Todd pedaled and at the same time leaned the opposite way from how the bike was tipping. It worked. The bike balanced again; he pushed hard and streaked across the finish line, his mouth curved into a big, surprised O.

Wow! He'd done it! My friend had done it, all by himself!

When Pinker gave Todd a fourth-place ribbon, the crowd, including Mom, Dad, and Rae Ann, cheered.

Yay, Todd!

Now everyone moved downfield to watch the trick riding. Everyone, that is, but Todd. He rode his bike to the building, parked it against the wall, then ran out to the grass where he'd last seen me.

"Here, boy!" he called. "Where are you? Please don't be lost!"

Poor Todd. He was so worried about me. Even though he seemed miles away, I ran after him. I wanted him to know I was okay. I wanted him to celebrate his bike ride.

I had almost caught up to Todd, and was out of breath, when Rae Ann appeared. "You were fantastic," she told him. "Now come on or you'll miss my trick riding."

"I can't," Todd said. "It's Bima. He's lost. I've got to find him right away."

"Oh, no," said Rae Ann. "I was afraid of this." She looked nervously at the far end of the course where the older kids were lining up. "I'll be disqualified if I don't get down there. Tell you what, come with me now, and as soon as I'm finished, I'll help you look for him."

"No," said Todd. "I have to find Bima."

With my sharp ears, I could hear every word of their conversation. Now, if I could just reach them in time—

"He probably buried himself in gravel or sand. Lizards do that, you know," said Rae Ann.

76

"Not when it's sunny and warm like today. He's out here somewhere," insisted Todd.

And moving toward you right now! I stopped and did ten push-ups, but they didn't see me.

"Bima! Bima!" Todd yelled in every direction.

Todd! TODD!

"This field is huge. He could be anywhere," said Rae Ann. She moved away from me again, and Todd followed her. "I think you should tell Mom and Dad. They'll help us find him."

Wait up, guys!

"I'll get in big trouble," said Todd.

"Bima's in trouble, too," said Rae Ann, starting to run. "We need Mom and Dad to help us. Come on, they're already down at the trick riding."

Todd was crying. "Okay, I'll tell them. Poor Bima!"

They headed down the field.

No! Don't leave me!

I collapsed. I was so tired from all that running. And so alone.

I was also overheated. Lizards can't sweat and cool off like humans. I needed a shade break to bring my body temperature down. I headed for the shadows of the school building.

On my way, I worried. Would I ever get home to my bedroom and my cozy cage again? Would I find Todd?

Would he find me? A puny lizard on a playground might as well be invisible. No doubt about it, I needed a miracle.

The next moment I saw it, leaning against the building. Straight ahead, a glint of silver, shining like a star. The Speedster!

Todd would have to come back to get his bike. And if I stayed near it, he'd come back to me, too.

I lay in the shade near the bike. At last, I could rest. I closed my eyes and dozed. Everything was going to be fine!

Or maybe not. What was this? The *crunch, crunch, crunch* of tennis shoes on gravelly asphalt? Who could it be?

I opened one eye and saw a familiar, ragged sweatshirt. Bobby! He was headed my way.

Okay, I told myself. Don't panic. Probably he just wants to ride the Speedster before Todd comes back. Probably he won't even see you. I waited still as a stone. Bobby ran closer and closer . . . until he passed the Speedster and me without a glance. He ran to a bench near the end of the building. Next to it lay his ruined bike. He kicked it again and again as if he wished it would fight back. Then he yelled, "Dumb old bike! Rusty old junk heap! I hate you! I hate you!"

With that temper, I was glad he hadn't noticed me.

No telling what he'd do to repay me for biting him. I backed farther into the shadows, and into a strange, new sound Bobby's yelling had covered up.

Chinkle-tink, it said. *Chinkle, chinkle-tink.*

I turned around and saw, creeping up behind me, something big. Something gray. Something with scraggly fur and a bell on its collar.

A cat! One swipe of her claw, and I would be lunch. She jingled closer.

Help, Todd! Help!

But Todd was far away. The cat would attack, and I wouldn't have a chance. I'd lost my friend, and now I was about to lose my life.

Chapter 10

All at once I remembered how I'd escaped the hawk. Faster than a lizard blink, I shinnied up the center bar of the Speedster. Sure, I knew I'd be scared and dizzy up there, but it was either that or be carried off in the cat's jaws.

The cat was on me in a flash, jingling all the way. She hunched under the bike, lifted one paw, and showed some claw. I hugged the center bar at the top, underneath the seat.

But the bike wasn't high enough. The cat snarled and jingle-stretched up to reach me easily. She was so close, I could smell mouse on her breath.

Then I heard someone run up to the bike. Todd had finally made it! I poked my head out to show him where I was, and saw . . . Bobby! I ducked back under the seat, caught between two enemies. I had to climb higher away from the cat. And Bobby, too. There. A window ledge just above me.

"Hey, you old cat," said Bobby. She hissed at him. "Hey," he said again. *Good. Keep him busy, cat.* Bobby still had not seen me.

A fast wriggle up the far side of the seat—*Don't look down! Up, up, up*—and I vaulted myself from bike to window ledge.

"Wow!" said Bobby. "A flying lizard!"

The cat howled and flashed her razor-paw. She missed me by a scale.

"Whoa," said Bobby. "Watch out, lizard!"

Had Bobby recognized me? I ran straight up the window glass. I ran from the cat, from Menlo, from everything that is out to get a lizard.

But it wasn't working. I slid backward down the slippery surface. Ran up again, slid down some more. Oh, for a chameleon's suction-cup toes that stick to anything! It was no use. The window glass was just too smooth for my claws to hang on to.

Bobby hissed at the cat. She hissed back.

I trembled and slid the last few inches down the window to the ledge. In the distance, I heard laughing, talking, the beeping of bike horns, and the squeaking of brakes. The victory parade! I'd almost forgotten about it. Maybe it would scare the cat away. Maybe . . .

Kitty glanced back at the parade and spit. Then

she turned her mean-green eyes on me and bared her teeth.

This was it. My last moment!

That's when everything happened at once: Kitty leaped, I tumbled backward off the ledge, falling, falling as Bobby yelled, "Look out!" and someone else caught me in midair.

"Bima!" Todd and Bobby cried together. Todd held me in one hand and swatted his free arm at the cat. She didn't budge. Bobby stamped his feet, then both boys yelled, "Aaarghhhhh!!" and it worked. The cat ran.

Todd cupped his other hand around me and said, "Bima, Bima, are you okay, boy? I'm sorry you got lost, so sorry. It was all my fault. Rae Ann was right. I shouldn't have brought you, but—"

I wished I had a handkerchief. Not for me, of course, but for Todd. Lizards don't cry.

Todd blinked twice and stared at Bobby as if he were seeing him for the first time. "Thanks," he told him. "Thanks for helping me get rid of that cat."

"Uh, sure," said Bobby. He turned to look at the parade. They were coming close. "We'd better get out of their way," he added.

"But we're gonna ride with them," said Todd. "It's the victory parade. Come on, get your bike."

"I don't have one. It fell apart after the relay race, re-member? It's totaled." Bobby pointed to the heap of broken chains and bent fenders.

"Then ride with me on my Speedster," said Todd.

Ride double? Are you crazy? No way you can pedal with Big Bobby on there. . . .

"But you ride in front," Todd told Bobby. "You're stronger. You can balance all three of us."

"You, me, and Bima," said Bobby. "Cool!" And he climbed on the Speedster with Todd and me sitting on the book rack behind him.

By this time, the parade of bikes had arrived. The kids slowed down and then stopped when they saw that Bobby and Todd were actually sharing a bike. They couldn't believe it. Everyone talked at once. "What's happening?" "Look, it's the lizard!" "Is he okay?" "What's he doing here, anyway?" "He came with Todd, dummy."

Erica wheeled over and smiled. "It's so cute that Bima came to the derby. He looks perfect in your pocket," she said. "Can I pet him?"

"Uh, sure, but be careful," Todd said. Erica touched the top of my head gently, and I nodded hello. I was glad she was not reptilophobic anymore.

Then Rae Ann found us. "Wow, Bima's here! And he's all right!"

Mom and Dad came running up. "Thank heavens!" said Mom, and Dad just smiled.

Rae Ann scratched me under the chin. "Why is Bobby—"

"It's okay," said Todd. "We're riding together now."

"Amazing," whispered Rae Ann.

Bobby said, "Come on, Boucher, let's roll. We're holding up the whole parade."

"Don't get lost ever again," Todd told me. He helped Bobby push off.

Don't worry. I'm not going anywhere.

"Guess what?" he asked me as we whistled along. "I came in fourth place in the obstacle course. I rode all by myself."

I know, I know!

"But you can ride with me anytime you want," he added generously.

Thanks, pal.

I stuck my head out of the pocket. As we skimmed along, waving parents took pictures. I gave Mom and Dad a big reptile grin.

That's when I remembered. Here I was, riding high. But I didn't feel nervous, not at all! I felt like a normal lizard scaling great heights. When I looked at Todd, I felt sure he and his family would always take good care of me. I'd never have to worry about heartless people like Scarp again.

We slowed, and the bike wobbled. "It's okay," Todd told me, helping Bobby to steady the wheels. "I've got it now."

You sure do, I agreed, snuggling against him. I felt like the luckiest lizard in the world.